Courted by a Cowboy

LACY WILLIAMS

ISBN: 1-942505-05-1
ISBN-13: 978-1942505051

ACKNOWLEDGMENTS

For Luke, my cowboy.

CHAPTER ONE

Wyoming, 1895

He'd arrived to grab his last chance by the horns, and he wasn't planning on letting go.

Sam Castlerock tied off his horse at the hitching post in front of the doctor's office and sauntered down the boardwalk in the small town of Bear Creek, Wyoming, toward his destination: the bank.

Late afternoon sunlight slanted over the roofs of the buildings lining the street; his boots thumped against the planks beneath his feet. Early summer had arrived—even here in town he could smell the buffalo grass from the surrounding prairie, and for a moment, he wished he was out riding the range. But he'd promised his father he would go through with this job and he would prove himself. He had to. Guilt was a powerful motivator, and it was high time he made things right.

From across the street, the exterior of the bank looked like every other business his father owned. Prosperous and elegant, with plate glass windows and gold lettering showing the name Bear Creek Bank. From the outside, the bank looked perfect. But looks could deceive. The bank was losing money.

And Sam was here to discover why. His father suspected the bank manager was letting delinquent loans slide, not following up on collection. He'd instructed Sam to find out if the man was doing it for his own gain or if he was just a bad businessman. Sam was ordered to use whatever means necessary to get the overdue loans collected—including calling in the loans as necessary. His father wanted to see the Bear Creek Bank profits increase.

Sam had six weeks. If he could prove to his father that he had the business acumen to bring things around for the bank and that he hadn't wasted three years of his life as a cowboy, his father would welcome him into the family business. And Sam would be able to make up for the mistakes of his past.

As a teen, Sam had longed for attention from his busy father, but had gone about getting it in the wrong ways. He'd run wild with a couple friends, played pranks and defaced property in his hometown of Calvin, Wyoming. He'd even attempted to steal a horse.

His actions had resulted in losing his father's esteem. He was blessed that his sister Penny had met and married an honorable man in Jonas White, who had taught Sam about being a cowboy, a real man—and respecting himself.

Now, after three years of cowboying, Sam had been given a chance to get back what he'd thought lost to him—his father's respect. It was the one thing he wanted more than anything else.

He wasn't due to report to the bank manager until tomorrow morning, but there was no reason he shouldn't introduce himself to the employees this afternoon before he rode out to his sister and brother-in-law's homestead outside of town.

He'd crossed the street and was reaching for the heavy, double-paned door when it burst open and he found himself with an armful of soft, fragrant woman. A crown of honey-colored hair brushed his chin as he fought to keep his balance, finally planting his feet and steadying her with a hand under both her elbows.

"Excuse me—"

"Emily?" They spoke at the same time, and her head jerked back when he said her name, revealing the hazel eyes that had haunted his dreams for longer than he wanted to admit.

"Sam!"

"Emily Sands. It is you." He backed away from the bank,

drawing her along with him several paces down the boardwalk.

She was prettier than he remembered—and he'd done a lot of remembering on lonely nights in his bedroll with only cattle and the night sky for company. Back when he'd spent summers in Bear Creek, working for his brother-in-law, she'd been off-limits, his best friend Maxwell's gal. But he'd never forgotten her, not in the two years since he'd seen her last.

"What are you doing here?" She ducked her chin but not before he saw the sparkling moisture pooled in her eyes.

His gut clenched, and his eyes automatically flicked to the gold-lettered windows behind her. Had she had trouble in the bank? "Is everything okay?"

She didn't quite meet his eyes. "Just taking care of some business. You didn't answer my question. What are you doing in Bear Creek?"

"I'm working for my father. At the bank." He waved a hand at the building and she looked up at him curiously, this time finding a smile.

"That's wonderful for you. Last time I saw you, you and your father weren't getting along so well."

He rubbed the back of his neck with one hand. That hadn't changed so far. He hadn't done the job yet. But he would. He wasn't going to disappoint his father this time.

~ * ~

Sam Castlerock was the last person Emily had expected to see—and possibly the answer to her prayers.

If he was working with the bank, maybe he could find a way to help with her family's situation. An overdue mortgage on the Sands' Mercantile and decreased sales due to hard times in this area had been plaguing her thoughts the past several months. That and her younger sister, Winnie.

Maybe Sam could put in a good word for her. Get the banker to offer her an extension. She would have to find the right moment to ask him. Sam had been a good friend in the past, and perhaps she could utilize that friendship to her benefit.

The man before her didn't look like a banker. He looked like a cowboy, from the auburn curls peeking out beneath his Stetson to his scuffed and worn boots. His broad shoulders looked as if they could carry a girl's burdens if she needed it.

If she was the kind of girl that believed in relying on someone to that extent. Which Emily wasn't. Not after the past two years of hard work, keeping her family afloat after her mother's death.

Back when Sam had been working as a cowhand for his sister and her husband, she and Sam had been friends, along with Maxwell White, one of their adopted sons. The three of them had been close, up until Maxwell had left for college and Sam had made an unexpected departure.

He hadn't even taken the time to say goodbye, and for weeks afterward, Emily's emotions had ranged from surprise to shock to anger. And then when her mother had passed away from an unexpected illness shortly thereafter, Emily had grieved the loss of the friendship—she'd needed someone to lean on. She'd been utterly alone, charged with the responsibility of caring for a challenging younger sister and keeping her father from drowning in his own grief.

But Sam was back now. Working for his father and the bank. Perhaps she could put the past to rest, and maybe Sam was the solution she needed to save her family's business.

"You headin' home? I'll walk with you."

Emily shook herself free of the thoughts swirling through her head. Sam waited with a patient smile, a flash of white teeth against his tan.

"Back to the shop, actually, to help my father close up." She could only hope Winnie hadn't destroyed any of the displays this time. Emily hated to leave her sister with her absentminded father, but she'd had no choice when she needed a private audience with the bank manager.

Her family's store was on the opposite side of the street, about halfway down, and her feet turned that direction of their own accord. Sam followed, extending his arm for her to take hold of.

"It's only a few blocks," she protested, but he raised his brows at her—a look she well remembered—letting her know that he wouldn't take "no" for an answer.

She slipped her hand into the crook of his arm and was surprised by the jolt of awareness that traveled up her arm. If he felt it, he didn't let on, keeping his gaze focused ahead.

"So you're still helping out in the store." His words were more of a statement than a question, but she nodded.

"Each and every day." Sometimes she felt like she was married to the store. For someone who'd dreamed of a family of her own, reality was a cold companion. She shrugged off her melancholy with an effort. "And you're working for your father. No more being a cowboy?"

He shrugged, eyes squinting a little beneath the brim of his Stetson. "I've got a chance to join the family business. Make things right with my father. Do my duty, as it were." He grinned.

She could understand family duty, too well. She hoped Sam's efforts paid off better than hers had so far.

~ * ~

"So Emily Sands is still in town?" Sam asked his friend Oscar White, later that night.

He made his words as casual as possible and didn't look up from tucking a faded quilt around his temporary bunk in the Whites' bunkhouse. Penny wouldn't hear of him staying at the boardinghouse in town, and while it would mean a longer ride for him each morning and evening going to and from the bank, he was secretly pleased. He loved his sister. It was because of her that he'd been enfolded into the White family.

Oscar lounged on the next bunk over, but looked up with a sharp-eyed gaze at Sam's words. All of the White boys had lived in the much-expanded cabin until Jonas and Penny's first baby had come along four years ago. Then the older boys had begged to be given their own space. Now the oldest three at home, Oscar, Edgar and Davy, stayed in the bunkhouse. And with Maxwell away at college, Sam took his friend's bunk.

Oscar made a noise in the affirmative, and that was all. Not enough information for Sam.

"She courtin' with anyone?" Sam couldn't stop the words, even though he risked merciless teasing from his friend.

"Not that I know of. Why? You interested?"

More than his friend could know. Seeing Emily again this afternoon had stirred all Sam's old feelings to new life. Just walking down the sun-lit street with her on his arm had made him want all kinds of things he shouldn't have wanted.

He avoided Oscar's question. "What about Maxwell?"

"What about him?"

"He used to be sweet on her." It was the reason Sam had left Bear Creek so quickly two years ago. He couldn't bear to be around Emily—be falling in love with her—when she belonged with his friend. It'd killed him to leave, but if he'd tried to explain she would've seen right through his excuses and known what a sorry friend he was.

"Far as I know, they cut ties when he left for college. He hasn't mentioned her in any of his recent letters."

For a moment, Sam allowed himself to hope. If Maxwell had no claim on Emily, then maybe Sam could have a chance to win her heart.

And then he thought about how very private his best friend was. If Maxwell still had feelings for Emily, he wasn't likely to put it in a letter—especially not one that his ornery brothers would read and josh him about. Sam *couldn't* be sure Maxwell was over Emily.

And Sam had a job to do. He didn't have time for entanglements if he was going to prove himself to his father. The best thing to do would be to keep his distance from Emily while he finished the job for his father.

CHAPTER TWO

Two days later, Emily had gathered her courage to speak to Sam about her family's mortgage. She left the mercantile early for lunch—leaving her sister at the shop with her father twice in one week—and rushed home to grab the picnic basket she'd put together early that morning.

When she arrived at the bank, she found Sam bent over the desk in the corner office, one elbow propped on the desktop and his hand thrust into his mop of auburn curls.

She knocked softly on the doorframe, and his head came up. His vivid blue eyes, the same color as the summer sky, brightened noticeably when he glimpsed her. "Emily!"

He stood and started around the desk, eyes crinkling in a smile. His greeting was warm, probably warmer than she deserved when she'd come to ask him for a favor.

But she pasted on a smile and lifted the wicker basket over her arm. "You look as if you could use a break for lunch. Want to go for a picnic with me?"

Her courage faltered when he hesitated, looking over his shoulder to the desk and the mess of papers strewn across it haphazardly. "I should..."

His halfhearted murmur started her heart beating again. He wanted to go with her. But maybe he thought he shouldn't leave his work undone?

"It's not going to disappear if you take a lunch," she said. She had experience with such things...at her family's store, there was always one more thing to be accomplished, one more order to complete or shelves to stock. It didn't end and likely never would.

His stomach rumbled, and he glanced up sheepishly from beneath his eyelashes, prompting her to laugh. He chuckled along with her, then gazed at her for a long moment with those blue eyes. Finally, he seemed to come to a decision. Something loosened in the set of his shoulders, and he scooped his Stetson off a credenza against one wall before joining her at the door and reaching for the coarse blanket she'd folded over her opposite arm. She released it to him, knowing he'd argue with her if she didn't.

"You've convinced me. Where should we go?"

"There's a pretty spot over near the church." It was on the edge of town and should be quiet. Few people would be passing by on a weekday, which meant fewer people to witness Emily's embarrassing attempt at asking for favor.

"Lead the way, friend."

Did he still consider her a friend? After he'd left so abruptly two years ago, without even a goodbye, she didn't know what to think. But she wasn't going to let that stop her, not when her family needed his help.

They walked together through the bank, passing the two bank tellers, who looked on curiously, almost enviously. Emily supposed they must find Sam as handsome as she did, but Emily wasn't going to risk her heart on someone who could just up and leave. She couldn't afford to, not with her responsibilities at home and her father's shop.

Outside, Sam used his free hand to reach up and loosen the tie at his neck. Even with the tie, white shirt under a dark vest and dark trousers he wore, she couldn't see him as a banker. He was still a cowboy to her. The boots he wore thumped on the boardwalk, proving her point.

"Have you been surviving office work?"

~ * ~

That was the question, wasn't it?

Sam was beginning to think he might not make it to the end

of the six weeks his father had asked of him.

After only two days, he was chafing for the physical labor he'd grown used to working with cattle and horses. Looking at ledgers and papers all day was fine and all, but there was a certain feeling you'd *accomplished* something when you lay down at night with aching muscles and blisters on your palms.

"I'm doing all right, I guess," he told her as they passed by a leather goods store.

Emily waved to the proprietor who was inside adjusting the boots in his window display.

Her presence had definitely raised his spirits. When he'd looked up to see her in the doorway, looking pretty as a picture in a light pink dress and with those bright hazel eyes, his heart had bucked like a colt under its first saddle. He'd hesitated to join her, but the thought of staying in the office through lunch and staring at more papers had depressed him.

He could use a friend. And Emily had been that for him in the past. He just had to keep his heart from getting too involved.

"How're things at the store?" he asked, to keep his mind from going down dangerous avenues. He knew Emily's father had a mortgage on the mercantile, had seen the overdue notation in the ledgers. She might not even know about it, depending on how much her father shared with her about the business.

As they walked, he reached out to grasp her elbow and help her step over a broken plank in the boardwalk, doing his best to ignore the feeling of vertigo resulting from his action.

"Mmm. Well, things haven't been easy over the last two years." She tilted her head as she looked up at him, her hazel eyes taking his measure. "After mother died..."

Her voice faded, and Sam squeezed her arm where it rested in his. "Maxwell told me, in one of his letters. I'm sorry." He'd tucked the knowledge away in a corner of his heart where he kept all the tidbits Maxwell—or anyone—mentioned about Emily. At the time, only weeks after he'd left Bear Creek and Jonas's spread, he'd had to fight the urge to return, to help

Emily in any way he could. He'd known, even then, that his actions would reveal the full depth of his feelings for her, and he hadn't been able to risk it. He'd asked Penny to pass on his condolences instead. And still regretted that he'd handled things that way.

Her eyes flicked away, and she nodded at the newspaper building across the street. "It isn't as if my family is the only ones who have suffered. The couple who owns the newspaper lost their son several months ago to a flooded creek. He was about same age as your sister's girl, Breanna. It really hit them hard, and they nearly lost the paper—until several of their neighbors took over running things until the worst of their grief passed."

Sam made what he hoped was an appropriate noise. He'd seen the note on the newspaperman's overdue loan just that morning. Seemed he would need to tread carefully when he went to talk to the man about it.

"And the druggist," Emily went on, pointing to a different storefront down the street. "Is actually a grandfather who took on the care of his five grandchildren when his daughter and her husband passed away last year. I can't imagine how he must have to make each penny stretch to feed that many children. So we aren't the only ones who have been struggling."

Emily's compassion for her fellow residents was touching. From their shared past, Sam remembered how sensitive she'd been to Maxwell's upbringing, helping him with the studies Penny had put him through, bringing him small treats from the store that he'd never gotten to have during his childhood.

Emily was like that, thoughtful to the needs of others. But who took the time to care about her?

"Oscar said you haven't gotten out to many social functions recently, been stuck in the store a lot," he said, as a way to broach the subject.

She glanced at him again, this time with eyebrows creased. "You were asking about me?"

He shrugged, his ears burning. "Just curious about an old friend." Mostly.

As they stepped off the end of the boardwalk, he tugged on the front of his Stetson, hoping it shadowed his face in case he was doing something as girly as blushing. He focused his eyes on the church steeple half-hidden behind a grove of trees up ahead but still felt her gaze on him.

Finally, she said, "My father hasn't been the same since my mother's death. She was almost a... partner to him in the store. When she died, it was as if he couldn't perform all those functions without thinking about her, so I took over a lot of it. And there's Winnie to take care of, as well."

That's right. He'd only met Emily's younger sister two or three times when he'd been in Bear Creek before, but it hadn't taken him long to figure she was a little different, a little slow. A sweet girl, but he imagined it took extra time and care to raise someone like Winnie.

"But, like I said, don't feel sorry for me. There are a lot of folks in Bear Creek who've been having a hard time of it."

They'd passed the last business but hadn't reached the church yet. Sam paused and wheeled around to look back down Main Street.

"There are a lot of folks behind on their payments at the bank, it seems," he said idly, trying to look at the town through unbiased eyes. There was plenty of foot traffic on the street, wagons traveling along, shoppers about.

And Jonas's homestead seemed to be doing well, from what Sam could see in the evenings. His herd was growing, and he'd been buying up additional land when each of his sons gained their majority. Sam knew not everyone was in the same position as his brother-in-law, but...

"I just don't see how people can't meet their obligations," he said.

She inhaled a quick breath and he looked down at her, but her head was bent and he couldn't read her expression. She clutched the basket handle with both hands.

"You've worked the range enough to know what some of the residents go through," she said the words a little sharply, surprising him. "With last year's bad drought, some of the homesteaders lost stock animals. The deep freezes this past winter took the winter wheat. There was also a wildfire a few weeks ago that destroyed several homesteads." Her voice grew softer, but she still didn't look up at him. "I don't think it's that people don't want to pay their loans. But if it's a choice between feeding your family or paying the bank..."

She still didn't mention her father's loan and Sam couldn't be sure that she knew about it. She could simply be sharing about the people she knew around town. If her father wanted to keep it private, who was Sam to bring it up?

"I'm sure you're right," he said, although he wasn't entirely sure of any such thing. "It's just...my father's counting on me to collect on the delinquent loans for the bank here. That's one of the major reasons he sent me." He didn't mention that collecting on those would make the bank more profitable.

"If what you've said is true, though, then how am I supposed to collect from people who can barely take care of themselves?"

His father would tell him to call the loans. But Sam didn't know if that was the right thing, either. He shrugged, looking off into the distance, into the sky past the town. His father was counting on him to prove that he wasn't the irresponsible person he'd been as a teenager. Prove that he was a man who finished what he started. He couldn't let his father down. But could he really look someone in the eye and tell him he was repossessing his property?

Emily seemed more subdued now than when she'd arrived at the office. Probably bored, talking business with him. Sam didn't even want to think about it anymore, and it certainly wasn't her problem.

He touched her arm. "So where is this perfect picnic spot?"

She seemed to come out of her thoughts, finally looking up at him. But her smile stayed restrained. She inclined her head toward the church. "Over there, beneath that largest oak."

He followed her, spreading the blanket where she wanted it. The spot overlooked a sunny meadow, enclosed by a plank-rail fence. Inside, a mare and her young colt grazed. Sam propped a boot on the lowest rail and watched the horses while Emily set out the food.

He breathed in deeply of the fresh, sun-kissed air, and some of his tension floated away on the breeze that rustled the nearby grasses. With the mountains in the distance and the bright sunlight streaming down, it made a pretty picture. The only thing that would make it better would be if he had his horse saddled and could race over the gentle hill to see what lay beyond.

And maybe if Emily rode behind him, arms wrapped around his waist.

The errant thought startled him into turning to face her. He leaned back against the fence, resting his elbows there.

With her honey-crowned head bent over her task and the dappled sunlight beneath the tree kissing her profile, she was even nicer to look at than the horses. He cleared his throat.

"So you don't have time to court because of helping your father run the store—but is there anyone special you've been seein'?" He hadn't really meant to utter the question, but maybe if she said yes, the cinch squeezing his chest would ease.

"No, there's no one like that." She said the words absently, setting one more item from the basket onto the blanket, then looked up at him and waved him toward her.

Heart bucking again, he joined her on the blanket, tossing his Stetson onto the soft grasses next to him.

"Have you heard from Maxwell recently?" He had to know.

She handed him a plate piled with delicious-smelling foods. "I get a letter every now and again but haven't for months. We'd gone from being sweethearts to friends even before he left for college."

So she counted Maxwell a friend. That answered how she felt about him, but what if Maxwell still carried a torch for her?

"What you said... about people paying their loans?" Her change in the topic surprised him momentarily. "I think if you get to know some of the Bear Creek residents, you might change your opinions about us."

He started to protest—he didn't think she or her father

were the kind of person who left a debt unpaid, but she kept speaking.

"Next Saturday, almost everyone in town is coming out to help the Bradfords re-build the house they lost in the wildfires. You should come. Meet some of the people. See what we're all about. Maybe getting to know some folks will help you figure things out."

Maybe it would. And maybe it wouldn't. He still had a job to do. Still had to prove himself to his father. But maybe the event would give him a chance to speak to some of the residents about paying their loans in a casual setting—one where they wouldn't be as offended as if he approached them in their own homes.

And maybe he could use the chance to make sure Emily was truly all right. It sounded like things had been difficult for her since her mother's death. He'd like to find a way to make things easier on her.

He could only pray for a way to do that without entangling his heart more.

CHAPTER THREE

"When I invited you to attend the house-raising, this wasn't exactly what I had in mind."

Emily's soft-spoken words seemed to drift off into the early morning darkness. The sun was still only a hint of silver light on the horizon as they made their way to the Bradfords' property outside of the town proper.

"I can't believe your father would let you make a delivery like this on your own," Sam countered. He glanced behind him at the over-full wagon, stacked with heavy lumber. The movement shifted his shoulder against Emily's on the narrow wagon bench, and he became aware all over again of her closeness, the way she pressed into his side. With the darkness surrounding them, it gave the moment an intimate feel.

He squinted his eyes, trying to see over the horses' ears in the darkness. Though he held the reins loosely, he could feel the horses straining in their traces with the effort to pull the heavy wagon. And Emily's father would have let her drive the wagon alone, if Sam hadn't insisted on doing it for her.

"It isn't the first time, and I doubt it will be the last," she murmured.

"You're not a freighter."

She didn't respond to his mumble, only jostled his elbow with a hint of a smile, a flash of white teeth in the growing light. "Besides, my father will be bringing the second wagon, along with Winnie."

It wasn't the first time he'd had a suspicion her father took advantage of her, worked her too hard. In the past ten days,

Sam had taken to riding past the Sands Mercantile on his way into town. No matter the early hour, he often saw Emily through the window, straightening or stacking or sometimes sweeping off the boardwalk outside. Almost always with her sister at her side. And when he rode home, often as twilight fell, she was still there. Still working.

Other than the picnic lunch they'd shared, he rarely saw her leave the shop during the daytime hours. So he'd taken to stopping by on his own lunch break. Sometimes he would bring by a treat from the café or hotel restaurant. Most of the time, he just tried to make her smile. He'd even gotten used to Winnie's often awkward presence and had found ways to relate to the younger girl.

Each time he saw Emily, his feelings grew. He was beginning to drift into dangerous territory—at risk of falling in love with her again. He couldn't let that happen. Not only was Sam convinced that it was possible Maxwell still had feelings for her, but she seemed determined to keep him firmly in "friend" territory—treating him the same as any of the White brothers who might happen into the store.

But he was resolved to stick it out. Emily had reached out to him those first two days when he'd been struggling sitting in the banker's office. It still wasn't easy for him to be confined to the desk all day, but her insights had helped him think about relating to the customers in a better way. She'd been a friend to him, and he could do no less for her.

He hadn't found time yet to approach her father about the overdue loan. Maybe he could catch a moment with the man today.

"I can't believe you slept outdoors last night. You should've slept at the store—I'm sure father wouldn't have minded."

He rubbed one palm over the scruff on his jaw. He probably looked a lot more like a cowboy today with unshaven cheeks and slightly-rumpled clothes, but he'd been afraid she would try to leave without him, wrestling the large, overburdened wagon on her own if he hadn't been there in time, so he'd spent the night beneath the same tree where they'd had their picnic, his horse ground-tied nearby. He'd been lucky to find out about the planned trip when he'd wandered into the shop late yesterday afternoon, and made his plans from there.

"It's plenty warm this time of year. It's no worse than when I'm out on a cattle drive. In fact, I kept coming awake, expecting to hear cattle lowing and was surprised to realize where I was."

She laughed. "I've been wondering if you were missing your cowboy days. I guess if you were dreaming about cattle, I've got my answer."

He chuckled with her but then admitted what he hadn't said to anyone else. "It's not only that. Being stuck in that stuffy office all day... it starts to wear on me by mid-afternoon. My legs get twitchy, and I get this urge to get on my horse and go for a ride. Get into some wide-open spaces."

He missed being out of doors. Missed the challenge of outsmarting wily critters and the need to keep ahead of the ever-changing weather. The travel from one spread to another, long cattle drives, and not having a place of his own, he could do without.

But if he couldn't complete this job, prove himself to his father, he would never earn his father's respect.

"There's something to be said about settling down. Having a place of your own to call home. And someone to come home to," he murmured.

~ * ~

Something in Sam's words hinted at a deeper meaning, and Emily's heart thumped sharply.

Maybe it was her imagination, but she thought she heard a wistful note there.

"Yes, but that doesn't mean you have to give up what you love," she argued. "If you'd rather work outdoors, why not settle your own homestead? Or work horses for a while with your grandfather until you decide what you want to do?"

The sun had finally tipped the horizon, and Emily could see the silent struggle cross Sam's features. "Maybe," he finally said. "After I finish with the Bear Creek Bank."

She wished she knew why this job for Sam's father was so important to Sam. He was a man of honor, and she expected no less than him giving it his all. He worked nearly as many hours in the bank as she did at her father's store—practically sunup to sundown. But what was he trying to prove?

She'd chickened out on asking him for an extension on her family's mortgage on the day they'd shared their picnic. He'd been so adamant about his job and making things right and so critical of those who couldn't pay their loans.

She hoped that by meeting some of the Bear Creek residents today, he would see they were real people with real struggles. If he could find compassion for them, maybe he would be more open to her request. She was running out of time. They were already overdue on the next loan payment. Her father had mentioned going to Sam to talk man-to-man, but Emily had put him off. She was Sam's friend. The request should come from her.

"What do you want to do with your life?" he asked.

It was only fair for him to turn the tables on her after she'd asked, but the honest answer was... "I don't know."

She couldn't see beyond her family's financial troubles. And even if they did find a way to save the store, there was Winnie to consider. Emily's sister was more like a child than a teenager. Emily's middle sister Marjorie had married and moved away, so there was no one else to share the burden with.

"Seems like you and Maxwell always talked about having a passel of kids that you'd take care of while he doctored the town."

"I can't believe you remember that," she said. "It seems like a long time ago."

It wasn't the first time Sam had brought Maxwell into their conversations. She was surprised he remembered so much about the time they'd spent together over two years ago now, she and him and Maxwell. By the time Maxwell had left for college, the romance between them had faded. Both she and Maxwell had realized the sparks from their teenage years had gone, and that what remained was a strong friendship—probably not the romance Sam was imagining they'd had. Sometimes, she'd thought perhaps *Sam* had had feelings for her. The occasional glance she would meet when he hadn't thought she would be looking...

"So... do you still want to have a passel of kids?"

She laughed, because it was either that or fight off tears. Having a family of her own was one of her most closely held dreams, but she didn't see how it was possible with her mother gone and her father and sister needing her so very badly. "I don't know. I suppose I'd like to have children someday. Why, are you offering?"

He coughed abruptly, jarring her elbow and rocking the wagon seat beneath them.

"I—" He spluttered and she laughed.

Although, all of a sudden, the thought of having Sam Castlerock as her husband didn't seem quite so funny.

~ * ~

"Watch your toes!"

Sam heard the cry moments before the wide plank would've smashed into his feet and was able to jump back out of the way.

"Sorry," Oscar called out, approaching. The other man swept off his hat and wiped his brow with a red kerchief. "Thought I could handle it. Where's your head, anyway?"

Sam shrugged, glancing over at the long tables where the womenfolk were laying out lunch for the men. Emily was there, bouncing a baby on her hip, smiling and talking with the women, Winnie at her side.

"Oh, I see." Oscar lined up shoulder-to-shoulder with Sam and nodded. "No wonder you're so distracted. Miss Emily's a sight. Especially with that baby on her hip. Could make a man start getting ideas about courtin'... or marriage."

Sam turned his back, purposely knocking his friend's elbow. "Too busy to be getting ideas like that," he mumbled. "C'mon. Let's get this board in place."

Oscar followed suit as Sam hefted one end of the board and put it in place against the home's outer wall. The house was taking shape beneath the hands of the workers who had shown up—almost all the town, it seemed.

"You sure? Seems like you've been distracted all morning."

Sam couldn't deny it. He'd had trouble keeping his gaze—and his mind—from wandering to Emily all day. Watching her interacting with the women, often reaching out to squeeze someone's arm, or interacting with the baby, looking natural and motherly—it cinched him around the middle and wouldn't let go. He knew it was wrong to want to be with her, but he couldn't help his feelings. When he completed this job for his father, he'd been promised a position but doubted it would be with the Bear Creek Bank. He could just imagine his father asking him to take on a business in Calvin, where his parents lived. To keep an eye on his son. Before coming to Bear Creek, Sam had seriously considered a position like that, even though he'd rather be riding the range. He'd do it to please his father, and ease his own guilt for the vandalism and pranks he'd pulled as a teen.

But now that Emily had started putting ideas about homesteading in his head, now that he was starting to imagine what it might be like to partner with someone like *her*... Sam was in an awful conundrum.

"You got your end?" he asked Oscar, hefting one side of the heavy board. Sam stuck several nails between his lips—both to secure them until he needed them and to keep from having to answer any more of his friend's questions.

He'd braced one hand against the board and was taking his first swing when the heavy plank slipped from his grasp.

"Gotcha!" A pair of hands braced it before it could fall.

Sam looked up to find himself shoulder-to-shoulder with the man Emily had pointed out when they'd first arrived.

"Jim Bradford," he introduced himself, before turning to greet Oscar at the other end of the board. "Morning, Oscar."

"Jim."

Sam pounded the nails with ease this time, the extra pair of hands helping enormously.

"You riding in the Calvin Round-Up next month?" Jim asked Oscar. Sam had forgotten about the cowboy event, that would feature men from all over Wyoming, Montana and Colorado. Maybe even draw some from Texas. Oscar was one of the best bronc riders around and supplemented his income with winnings from traveling to different competitions when he wasn't helping Jonas on the spread.

"Yep, that's the plan," Oscar said before Jim moved down to support his end of the plank.

"Wanted to thank you boys for coming out today—it means a lot to me."

Oscar mumbled something around the nails in his teeth.

"And a special thanks to you," Jim said, nodding to Sam, "for helping Miss Emily with delivering that first load of lumber. It was a kind thing to do when you don't even know us."

Heat burned Sam's ears beneath his hat. He'd wrestled that wagon out to this homestead for Emily—hadn't even spared the homeowner a thought. He cleared his throat. "Sure."

After Oscar had hung his end of the board, the three men worked together to do another, then moved aside when another pair of men brought several more planks and began hammering them up.

"It's shaping up," Oscar said.

Sam let his eyes roam the partially-complete building. The frame had been completed earlier, and men braver than Sam scaled the skeleton roof, securing the boards overhead. With two walls to go and some work on the interior, the house should be mostly finished by the end of the day.

"Yep. Alice and I are blessed indeed."

Sam glanced askance at the man beside him. Jim couldn't be much more than Sam's twenty years, if any. And they were surrounded by a burned out homestead. The devastation had been enough to make Sam gasp when he and Emily had pulled the wagon into the yard just after daybreak. Fields of blackened stubble, the house and barn burned out down to the very foundations. A pen of chickens had been the only sign of life until townspeople had begun to arrive, although Emily had said most of the livestock had run off ahead of the fires and survived.

The other man seemed to sense Sam's disbelief. "We got out," he explained further. "I don't know what I would've done if I would've lost Alice or little Annie."

Without work to keep him occupied, Sam's eyes wandered back to Emily, who now had her arm wrapped around her younger sister, bringing her into conversation with another young woman near the food tables. He could understand the fierceness in Jim's voice—if anything bad were to happen to Emily, Sam would never be the same.

Oscar slapped the other man on the shoulder. "Little Annie's getting so big. Couldn't believe it when I saw her toddling around this morning."

"I know it. And, well... we haven't told many folks yet, but there's gonna be another little one come winter." Now Jim's voice took on a slight undertone of worry.

Sam glanced around the homestead, trying to imagine how the man would support his family. His thoughts also flicked to the notation in the bank manager's ledger—Jim and his wife had mortgaged their place when times had been tough last year. Sam had planned to talk to the man about it today, but found he couldn't broach the subject now.

"Congratulations!" Oscar seemed to recognize the other man's anxiety and his levity faded to seriousness. Sam's friend could be serious when he tried. "You know the church will help out. My family as well."

"Thanks. Alice and I have been talking a lot—trying to figure out a way to keep from having to sell out and move back East, where her parents are." Jim shifted his booted feet. "Her pa never approved of me. I'm afraid if we had to move back and live off their charity, it would just get worse." He seemed to shake off his thoughts, and rolled his shoulders. "But that's probably more than y'all wanted to know. Looks like they need help unloading that second lumber wagon."

He started to walk away, before turning back to Sam. "I know we're behind on our loan. But we've got every intention to pay what we owe. I just wanted you to know that."

Sam reached out and Jim shook his hand. He liked the other man, couldn't help it. It was obvious he was a hard worker and cared about his family but had just fallen on hard times.

Those thoughts were dangerous to Sam's mission. Could he afford to feel this compassion for those who had taken out the loans he needed to collect on?

"C'mon. Let's grab another couple of planks and get to it." Oscar's thud on Sam's shoulder broke him out of his thoughts, and he followed his friend back to work.

CHAPTER FOUR

"Oh!" Emily's startled cry wasn't quick enough to stop the toppled glass or the spilled water that splashed onto Sam's trousers and the picnic blanket they shared with her sister Winnie.

"Winnie!" Emily's distress was tangible. "Oh, Sam, I'm sorry."

Winnie hummed and flapped her hands above her half-empty plate oblivious to her mistake. For a moment, Sam worried that her shifting feet would dislodge the picnic food laid out on the blanket between them, but everything remained in place as Emily tried to calm her.

Sam was disappointed for Emily's sake that their father didn't take more charge of the girl, but the times he'd seen Emily's father interact with Winnie, it seemed the man didn't know how to relate to his youngest daughter. And that left Emily with the majority of the burden of Winnie's care. But Emily didn't seem to regret her situation in the least. He'd never witnessed her lose her temper with Winnie, no matter how difficult the girl could be.

"Oh, Winnie, you've soaked your skirt." Emily used the towel that had been wrapped around a loaf of bread to dab at her sister's skirt and then the blanket. "Sam, you all right?"

Sam brushed at the small wet patch above his knee. It really wasn't bad. "It's fine, ladies." He winked at Winnie, who blinked at him with an owlish gaze. "A little water is the least of what these trousers have come across during my travels. Besides, it's warm enough out here—I'll be dry in no time.

Maybe Miss Winnie just thought I didn't do a good enough job washing off down at the creek before we sat down to eat."

"Sam!" Emily exclaimed, but her voice sounded more like a laugh and less like the tight squeak it had been a moment ago. "Well, I'm sorry anyway. Winnie, can you say 'sorry'?"

A faint blush brightened Emily's cheeks, and Sam wondered if she was embarrassed or expected him to be angry. He probably shouldn't have, but he closed his hand over hers, stilling her frantic blotting of the blanket. "It was an accident."

Her hazel eyes held his for a long moment, questioning. He let her look, enjoying the moment to study her beautiful face, hoping she saw whatever answer she was looking for in him. He liked her sister. The fact that she was a little different didn't bother him.

"Bird!" Winnie clucked, waving her hands again and breaking the connection between them.

Emily turned to murmur softly to her sister, calming the girl. Sam watched her unabashedly, fascinated by the pink stain still clinging to her cheeks. Her gentle way with a sister that many would find difficult to deal with spoke of her love for Winnie. And reminded him a little of his sister's patience with a difficult sibling—namely him when he'd been a teenager and drifting along without a purpose. Because of Penny, he'd met Jonas and because of the both of them he'd found God and found peace with himself. Emily's soothing presence was a reminder of the family he wanted—a wife and children who could love him unconditionally. Was there any way he could be sure of Maxwell's feelings?

He cleared his throat. "Worked with Jim for a bit earlier. He's... not what I thought he would be." He'd expected the man to avoid talking about the overdue loan, but he'd admitted it, and shared his concerns about his family and livelihood. Sam had liked the man.

"Before the wildfires, he spent time almost weekly helping some of the other homesteaders who had suffered with the winter freezes. Since then, he's been working night and day to try and salvage what he can on his own place."

Emily's gaze wandered to the pair, who played with their baby on a blanket not far away. Did she know how wistful she looked? Before Sam could comment, his four-year-old nephew Walt rushed onto the blanket, toppling Sam's empty plate from his knee and rattling the silverware. Two-year-old Ida toddled behind him, shrieking and reaching for Sam.

"Sorry—" Sam mumbled over an armful of toddler. "My niece and nephew."

"I know." Emily waved at Walt, who had gone shy and ducked behind Sam's shoulder. "Your sister brings them into the store occasionally." She pointed to a piece of chocolate cake on her plate, crooking her finger, and Ida sprang from Sam's lap to settle in Emily's.

Walt crept from behind Sam to perch on his knee, one finger stuck in his mouth. "Unca Sam, you gots cake?"

Emily made quick work of juggling both the toddler in her lap, the plateful of cake and dishing out Sam a chunk of cake from the platter at her side.

She was a natural, talking to Ida softly and holding the toddler's attention raptly, and even bringing Winnie into the interaction, so that the two sisters' honey-colored heads bent together.

Penny came and collected the kids after a few moments, staying only long enough to greet Emily warmly before she attempted to get them to nap in the shade of the White's wagon. When Emily turned back to Sam, he couldn't help his grin at the small chocolate handprint on her jaw.

He held up his kerchief, nodding to her cheek. "You've got a little..."

She bent toward him and he wiped the chocolate smear, but his efforts only made it worse.

"Here, scoot over—"

She moved slightly closer, until her knee pressed against his thigh. He dipped the kerchief in his mason jar of water and this time captured her chin in his fingers, holding her steady so he could get the cake off.

With the last remnants gone, he looked up, right into her

eyes. He couldn't make his fingers release her chin. What he really wanted to do was lean forward and kiss her. He even inched toward her, his Stetson brushing the wisps above her forehead.

Then Winnie squealed, breaking the moment, and he remembered where they really were. Surrounded by people. Although no one seemed to be paying them any attention, he would never shame Emily by kissing her in public.

Especially when he shouldn't even be considering kissing her at all.

~ * ~

Had Sam almost kissed her?

As the men returned to the house that was taking shape beneath their many hands, Emily settled her sister for a rest on their picnic blanket in the shade.

Her shaking hands and swirling thoughts were not so easily settled as she gathered their dishes to wash them out in the large tubs set up for just that purpose.

The way he'd looked at her so intently... his fingers warm on her jaw... She really thought he was going to kiss her. And she would have let him.

She pressed one hand against her stomach as butterflies threatened to displace the chocolate cake she'd enjoyed with Sam's niece.

Seeing him every day in the shop in the last week and a half had re-affirmed their friendship—and his gentleness and patience with Winnie had her wondering if she could be falling in love with the handsome cowboy-turned-banker.

Today, he'd seemed so much at ease. More a cowboy, with his broad shoulders straining beneath a chambray shirt, working alongside the men of town. And a little scruffy, unshaven after being outside all night. She'd seen him talking with Jim Bradford and Oscar and hoped that he would begin to understand that money wasn't everything—that the people were important.

She'd hoped to bring up her family's money situation on the wagon ride home. But with the emotions swirling through her at this very moment, Emily wasn't sure she should. Would Sam think she was exploiting what was growing between them—whatever this all-encompassing, heart-pounding emotion was?

Would she be manipulating what was between them?

And why did that thought squeeze her insides into a tiny, painful ball?

CHAPTER FIVE

Sam listened to the steady, even cadence of Oscar's voice as the other man worked an unbroken mare using a long line in the round corral.

"Easy, boy." He slung the saddle his friend had requested he bring from the lean-to over the corral railing and leaned on his elbows next to it, finding himself lulled by Oscar's manner with the horse.

Or maybe his sense of relaxation came from doing what he considered "real work," with his friend. Being out in the open, working the horses under the cloudless blue sky had a certain peace about it that he still couldn't find in the office at his father's bank. He'd felt the tension he'd carried for the last days start to fade the moment he'd decided to spend this beautiful Saturday working with Oscar instead of behind his desk.

"You bored yet, Mr. Banker?" Oscar's voice carried from inside the corral, even though he spoke in the same tone he'd been using to work the horse.

It was just the two of them in the corral Oscar had built across the valley from Jonas's place. Up the hill a ways was the nearly-finished cabin that Oscar planned to occupy. With the help of Jonas and his brothers, it had gone up the past spring, and Oscar planned to finish it this summer.

"No." Sam wasn't bored at all. He was wondering how he could finish out the remaining two weeks he'd promised his father. He'd made small inroads on collecting some of the overdue loan payments, something the bank manager apparently hadn't worked very hard on, but the bank was still a long way from making a profit.

He was coming to discover the difficulty of collecting the loan payments wasn't why he was chafing at the bank. He knew he could do a good job, given enough time. But Sam was beginning to think he wasn't meant to be a banker. He missed being outdoors. Missed working with his hands, and seeing the fruits of his own labors, not just collecting on someone else's labors.

And he didn't want to think about the bank today.

"Your place is taking shape," he commented, working to marshal his thoughts.

Oscar nodded, mouth curling with pride. "Another couple of wins in the summer's round-ups, and I'll be able to afford the stallion I've really been wanting. And if that doesn't play out, I've got a lead on a good-paying job for later this fall—a well-off rancher up north looking for a trainer for a fancy-pants colt he's got." Oscar sent a grin over his shoulder. "I'm anxious to get started with the breeding program I have in mind."

Sam let his eyes rove the herd of quality animals that grazed between Oscar's place and Jonas's. He'd heard about his friend's plans to raise horses since they'd known each other as teens. Oscar's dreams were all panning out, but Sam still didn't know what he really wanted to do with his life.

"Sounds like you've got it all planned out." Sam tried to keep the slight envy he felt out of his voice. "You'd better watch out though. Some gal's going to find out you've got this beautiful place built, a livelihood all ready to go. One of these days, someone is going to lasso you and haul you to the altar."

Oscar released the horse from the pattern he'd been running it through and turned to spear his friend with a look as sharp as a whip-crack.

"After seein' you with Emily at the house-raising, seems like getting hitched is what *you* really want."

And that was Sam's real problem. There was no denying it—he was falling in love with Emily Sands. And if her welcoming smiles the last couple of days were any indication, she might have growing feelings for him as well.

"So what's stopping you?" Oscar asked. "How come you're out here with me instead of courting your gal in town today?"

Sam scuffed the toe of his boot in the soft dirt. "You said before you thought Maxwell was over her. But your brother is a real private person. What if he still has feelings for her?"

Oscar's eyes narrowed. "If you really love her, you won't let a little problem like that stand in your way."

"But he's my best friend."

"And you're his. He would want you to be happy."

But how could Sam be sure?

~ * ~

With only one week left until the deadline his father had imposed, Sam should probably be spending the evening at the bank, trying to find a bit more profit for his formidable father, but when Emily had invited him to the housewarming party for the Bradfords, he hadn't been able to say "no."

Much of the crowd from earlier had dispersed, although several folks hung around in the yard, chatting. Sam had been impressed with the town's generosity, even from those who didn't have much. Each family had brought what they could—whether it was some newly sewn linens or the nice cast iron skillet Emily's father had sent along. With the gifts they'd received, the Bradfords wouldn't have an empty new house. Instead, it would feel like a home.

Sam and Emily stood at the washtub in the new kitchen, scrubbing the last of the supper dishes from the potluck.

"I saw that Jim had gotten his closer fields plowed and planted with a late crop," she murmured at his elbow.

Heat flushed his face as he anticipated her next words.

"Alice mentioned you'd been out two afternoons to help him get it done. I was wondering why I hadn't seen you ride out Tuesday and Wednesday evenings."

He shrugged it off. It hadn't been a big deal. Since working with Oscar, he'd been itchy to do more manual labor anyway.

Although part of him couldn't help but be pleased that she'd noticed his absence.

"It meant a lot to them," she continued, and this time she seemed to wait for a response, holding the dish he was attempting to take from her until he met her eyes.

His ears remained hot, but he said, "Jim shouldn't have to go crawling back to his father in order to support his family. And I didn't do much."

"Why it is okay for him to break ties with his father, but not you?" she asked. Over the last weeks, he'd told her a little about wanting to earn his father's respect, but not all of it.

The quiet swish of the water was the only sound between them for a long moment as he considered the best way to answer her. The truth.

"It's more than me just being estranged from my father for the past couple of years. Before that..." He swallowed hard. "You gotta understand that my father is a tough man. Strict. No nonsense. High expectations. As a teenager, I balked against the restrictions he put on me. All his rules felt like... like a noose choking me instead of something meant to protect me. I did lotsa stuff I'm not so proud of now. Got into trouble. Defaced personal property. Even tried to steal a horse once, although the marshal let me off easy on that one. Part of it was his rules, but part of it was... trying to get his attention, I guess. I wanted him to notice me. Not just as someone sitting across the kitchen table at breakfast, but for the person I was. I'm still trying to make up for those times. Still trying to get him to understand I'm not the boy I once was... I want to earn his respect."

She listened in silence, the dishes done, her face turned to his. *Truly* listening to him. When he was finished, flushed with shame, she reached out and touched his arm. Her touch seared him, even through his damp shirtsleeve.

"Sam, everyone's got regrets."

He gave her a skeptical look. Emily was one of the nicest people he knew. What did she have to regret?

But there were shadows in her eyes when she continued

speaking. "Until I was eleven years old, I resented Winnie deeply. She took so much of mother's time and attention—and she was so different from my middle sister Marjorie. She couldn't respond like other girls her age."

The self-deprecation in her voice stunned him. He'd seen the way she acted with her sister. The gentle, patient care she gave.

"I didn't even like her," she whispered. "But then..."

She released his arm, but he couldn't bear to lose the contact, so he claimed her hand.

"She came to school with Marjorie and I, even though she couldn't understand the lessons. And the other kids often picked on her. And that day, so did I. The things I said were so cruel, and I'm still deeply ashamed of them. She must've understood some of it, because she ran off in tears. I got in so much trouble at home..."

She shook her head. "But when I finally faced her after supper that night, it was as if she didn't even remember. As if she'd wiped my slate clean of the entire offense."

Now her voice trembled. "It was the first time I really understood the depth of God's love for his children—what He did for us by sending Jesus to die. And Winnie taught it to me, with her simple outlook on life."

She wiped her free hand beneath her eyes; it came away glittering with moisture. Sam squeezed the hand he still held in his.

"From then on, things have been different between us. But that's not my only regret—or even my deepest."

He waited, still holding onto her hand, hoping somehow that his presence could anchor her.

~ * ~

If she hadn't grown so much closer to Sam in the last weeks, Emily would never have found the courage to tell him what she was about to reveal. It was too personal—too private. She could only hope the feelings she saw revealed in his eyes didn't disappear when he realized what it meant.

"You remember when we first met—the summer that Maxwell and I courted briefly?"

He stiffened slightly, and his expression closed. Was he bothered by her reference to the previous courtship? Should she keep going? Could she?

"Before that, I'd been taking on more and more of Winnie's care at home. But I was tired of always having · to be responsible. I wanted some time for myself. So I planned a trip to see my aunt."

"I remember that," he said quietly.

"I thought that mother and my middle sister would be able to care for Winnie adequately, but she and I had grown so close... one afternoon they weren't paying attention and she burned her leg badly. We almost lost her," Emily whispered. "I didn't even find out until I'd returned home and she was bed-bound."

Even now, years later, the guilt threatened to swamp her. How could she have been so selfish? She'd put her own needs ahead of her sister's and look what had happened. Was it happening all over again? Was she being selfish? Letting her feelings for Sam overshadow what she should have asked him weeks ago—for help with the loan? If she mentioned it now, would he think she'd gotten close to him for the wrong reasons?

Sam must've sensed her emotion and confusion, because he tugged on her hand and drew her close. Emily's hands came to rest on his chest and she accepted the embrace, the comfort he offered. Tears burned her throat, but she had to say it all—finish it.

"You've teased me about wanting a family of my own, but Winnie is my family first. I can't ever let something like that happen to her again. With mother gone, it's up to me to ensure Winnie is cared for." She murmured the words into his shoulder, too scared to look up into his face.

Did he understand what she was trying to tell him? What that meant for the two of them?

He drew back slightly, tipped up her chin with his strong, calloused fingers. The way he looked at her...

"Sam," she breathed.

He hesitated, so minutely she might've imagined it, then bent his head and brushed his lips over hers.

His kiss was as gentle and sure as the man himself, and she clutched his shoulders, wishing he never had to let her go.

And then he was stepping back, turning away from her, rubbing a shaking hand over the back of his neck. She wanted to reach out to him, to recapture the closeness they'd shared just moments ago, but she was afraid. What if the things she'd shared with him had changed the way he felt about her?

Then her resolve firmed. No matter if she was falling in love with him, Sam had been a good friend to her. She could do no less.

~ * ~

He shouldn't have kissed her. He'd known it and had done it anyway. He hadn't been able to stop himself from bending those last few inches and tasting her lips.

And he found he couldn't regret it.

Emily's hand came to rest against the back of his shoulder, and he jumped. He forced himself to face her, even as he tried to put some space between them.

She didn't look upset. In fact, the firm set of her lips told him she was about to say something and that he might not like it. He braced himself.

"I had to find a way to forgive myself for what happened with Winnie—both times. And you've got to forgive yourself for rebelling against your father. Even if he never accepts your apologies, if things never fully resolve between you, forgiving yourself for the mistakes of the past is the only way you'll ever be free of it."

Penny had said something similar to him before, but he hadn't listened. Just continued on his quest to prove himself to his father, prove that he could be the son his father wanted.

Was he listening now because he *wanted* to be free of the hold his father had on him? Because he wanted to be free to pursue Emily?

He didn't know.

She'd given him a lot to think about—not the least of which was the kiss.

"We should head back to Bear Creek," he murmured, not ready to make a decision tonight. He'd been trying to earn back his father's respect for so long... he wasn't even sure he *could* let it go.

But with Emily looking at him with that soft gaze, he was inspired to try.

CHAPTER SIX

Sam stared at the ledgers in front of him, the names and numbers blurred to his eyes.

He couldn't stop thinking about Emily, about what had passed between them last night. There was no question he was in love with her.

The only question was what he should do about it. He'd been toying with the idea of sending Maxwell a letter all morning, declaring his feelings for Emily. He thought his friend would step aside, even if he had continuing feelings for Emily. Sam could only hope their friendship wouldn't be damaged beyond repair.

He had some savings from his cowboy days. Enough to give them a start but not much more. If she agreed. They needed to have a long talk to sort things out between them. He wanted to tell her that he would never keep her from caring for her sister. He wondered if he could get her to sneak away from the shop at lunch.

A sharp knock on the doorframe broke him from his thoughts and pulled his head up.

"Oscar. What're you doing here?"

"Had a little business in town and got a wire. Thought you might be interested in what it had to say."

His friend dropped a small square of paper on Sam's desk. Curious, he flicked a glance at Oscar before reaching out to pick it up.

"It's from Maxwell," Oscar said.

Heart pounding, Sam lifted the paper. "*Emily and I are just friends. STOP. Tell Sam he should risk it. STOP,*" Sam read aloud. He re-read the words once. Again. Realized his hand was shaking and then let the paper flutter to the desk, hoping his friend hadn't noticed.

"You did this?" Sam asked, finally looking up to a smug Oscar.

"Got tired of waiting for you to get off your laurels and do the chasing that girl deserves. Anyway, I got to get back to the homestead. Big round-up down in Laramie this weekend and I've got things to wrap up."

"Oscar." Sam's call halted his friend just before he got to the door.

Oscar turned, shoving his Stetson back on his head, a half-grin still in evidence on his face.

"Thanks," Sam said. "Someday I hope to return the favor."

His friend nodded and left.

Sam's eyes returned to the square of paper that set him free to follow his heart.

Then his eye caught on a line of handwriting on the ledger just below one corner of the wire. *Sands Mercantile.*

He used his thumb to slide the paper out of the way, following the line of writing across the page. He still hadn't spoken to Emily's father about the delinquent note. He'd been busy working with other customers... and once he'd started growing closer to Emily, he'd put it off, not wanting anything to come between them.

He immediately thought of all the times he'd complained to her about the people of Bear Creek who were behind on their loans. Was she embarrassed that her family was one of them? Did she think that he would think less of her because they'd hit a difficult time?

When he'd first arrived in town, maybe that thought wouldn't have been far off, but surely she could see how his attitude had changed since he'd gotten to know the people of Bear Creek.

Or maybe she didn't know it.

He had to talk to her, settle things between them. Now.

Emily was measuring yard goods for a customer when Sam pushed through the mercantile door, the little bell above tinkling to signal his entrance.

From the set of his jaw, she could immediately tell something had happened. She hurried her customer through selecting a matching ribbon and thankfully the store was empty of other customers.

He reached for her hands when she went to meet him, and that reassured her minutely.

"Can you spare a moment to talk?" he asked.

"Let me go tell papa—he's in the back taking inventory."

She joined him on the boardwalk, and he led her to a semi-private bench in the town square. He took her hand again once they'd sat down.

"Did you know about your father's loan? Why didn't you talk to me about it?"

Heat flooded her face. She forced herself to hold his gaze, even through the shame and humiliation.

"I... was going to. That first day when we picnicked, but I just... couldn't." She looked down at her lap, her eyes falling on their clasped hands, between them on the bench. He hadn't let go of her yet.

"You must've thought real highly of me, going on all the time about people not paying their loans." He shook his head, his Stetson casting his face into partial shadow. But to her surprise, he sounded more upset at himself than at her...

"It wasn't that. I was embarrassed about my family's situation, at first. Then... when you kept coming around ... I thought... I felt..." Now her face felt as if it were on fire. "We started getting closer, and I thought if I asked for another extension on the loan, that you'd think I was using you—or exploiting the feelings between us."

Admitting that she *did* have feelings for him made her almost afraid to look at him. Until he squeezed her hand and she found the courage to raise her chin and meet his gaze.

"What's between us is real." His vivid blue eyes were steady on her. "Em, I'll talk to my father, see what can be done about the loan. And I'll do whatever I can to ease things for your family."

Tears burned her eyes. She knew how much he wanted to do a good job to prove himself to his father. But Sam was saying he would take her side, her father's side. Maybe, just this once, she wouldn't have to bear things alone. Not with Sam behind her.

He tucked a strand of hair behind her ear, letting his fingers brush her cheek before resting his elbow on the bench behind her shoulder.

"I wish we were someplace alone," he said quietly. "I really want to kiss you again."

Her heart leapt.

"...But there's too many people out on the boardwalk, some of them watching us right now."

She ducked her chin into her shoulder. "I was under the impression you weren't sure you were happy you kissed me last night."

"I didn't regret it, if that's what you mean. I let myself get a little too caught up in the obstacles between us—and a little afraid that I'd fail you like I did my father."

He didn't say more, but she could read his sincerity in his face.

It made her brave enough to say, "Then maybe you should come by the house for supper tonight and take me for a walk afterward."

He smiled—that quicksilver grin she loved—but before he could answer, hurried footsteps on the boardwalk approached and someone called, "Mr. Castlerock!"

One of the bank tellers approached, looking chagrined that she'd interrupted them, but panting in her hurry.

"What's the matter?" Sam rose and drew Emily to her feet.

"Your father's here—at the bank."

CHAPTER SEVEN

Although Emily had offered to come with him to face his father, Sam had escorted her back to the mercantile and made his way back to the bank.

His father sat behind what had been Sam's desk until this point, fingers tracing over the ledgers open before him.

Sam cleared his throat from the doorway, but the elder Castlerock took his time in looking up, forcing Sam to wait.

Making him feel same as always, like a child interrupting something important. Finally, his father looked up, although he didn't rise from Sam's chair.

"Samuel."

Sam couldn't tell anything from his father's tone. Why had the man arrived early?

"I'm a little surprised to see you. I thought we were meeting on Monday."

"And I was likewise surprised to find you were out of the office. During the middle of the afternoon."

Sam straightened his shoulders against his father's disapproving tone. His actions were nothing to be ashamed of, especially in the light of the talk he'd just had with Emily. Although they hadn't made any formal declarations, she seemed to return his feelings. And that solidified the decision he'd been coming to over the last few weeks.

"I had to see a friend."

His father's eyes narrowed at the simple explanation, but Sam didn't offer more. He was a man now, whether his father wanted to admit it or not.

"Sit down." The elder Castlerock motioned Sam to a chair across the desk, his eyes already on the papers before him. "I had an important meeting rescheduled to early next week. So we'll go over your results today."

Of course he did. He hadn't given one thought that Sam might have other commitments or want to finish up anything before he made his report on the bank's profitability.

For a moment, Sam remained on his feet, fighting the urge to rebel against what his father wanted. In the face of his father's dismissive attitude, he almost wanted to walk out the door.

But he wouldn't. He'd committed to seeing this through, and he would.

His father tapped one of the open ledgers in front of him. "I can see that you've made a good effort at collecting the delinquent loans. Not what I'd hoped, of course, but more than I expected."

Bitterness welled, but Sam pushed it down. He might never be able to meet his father's expectations. But did it really matter, if he'd won the love of a woman like Emily?

"Some of the loans you've let slide... Why haven't you pushed harder on them? Look at this one... the mercantile? It's one of the worst overdue. If you'd called the loan weeks ago, at least we might've recouped some profits by selling off the assets."

Sam went hot and then cold. Of course his father would focus on the one thing Sam didn't want to bring up yet—not when things between he and his father were unresolved. But Sam had made the decision to wait on pursuing the Sands' loan, and he would stand behind it now.

His father steepled his hands in front of his rather portly belly, becoming more animated as he spoke. "They've probably got inventory that we could recoup funds from, not to mention the building. I'd have to look at the mortgage agreement, but if the home is listed as collateral, we could repossess it as well."

"And what about the family that you'd displace. What happens to them?"

His father shrugged. "They're the ones who got themselves into this situation."

It was bad enough that they could lose their livelihood, but Sam couldn't bear the thought of Emily being thrown out of her home. She had such a generous spirit, and even if her father could be a little absentminded and things in Bear Creek had been hard, she didn't deserve it. Sam wouldn't—couldn't—let that happen.

Sam stood, startling his father into finally looking at him, really looking. He clutched his Stetson against his thigh, praying that his father would really listen.

"I know we haven't always seen eye to eye and that I disappointed you a lot when I was a teenager. I don't guess I've ever asked your forgiveness for that and I know I probably don't deserve it anyway."

His father didn't look away. He didn't say a word, but Sam sensed that he had his attention—for once.

He went on. "I've figured out some things since I've been working here in Bear Creek. I'd like to show you, if you'll go with me." He extended one hand toward the door, waiting for a long, tense moment while his father considered him. Finally, his father stood.

His father remained silent, but accompanied Sam first to the mercantile, where his eyebrows almost disappeared beneath the brim of his bowler hat when Sam introduced him to Emily and asked her to accompany them.

She wore a similar wide-eyed expression, but spoke briefly to her father before joining them on the boardwalk. Sam captured her hand and tucked it into his arm, turning in the same direction of that first eventful picnic they'd taken together, just after his arrival in Bear Creek.

"Em, I know you've told me the story of the people who own this business before, but I wasn't really listening back then. I'm listening now. Will you tell it again?" Sam pressed Emily's hand with his fingers, encouraging her to speak with a nod at the newspaper building.

She repeated the story about the couple who had lost their

son to a flooded creek, and how their neighbors had helped run the business for months until they'd come out of their grief. Sam took his father inside to meet the couple, who were effervescent in their thanks that the bank had extended their loan.

Then Emily accompanied them to the druggist's shop, where the elder Castlerock met the grandfather who'd taken on his five grandchildren. He, too, was thankful to Sam's father for allowing him and his family to stay on their feet with the bank's generosity.

And as they returned to the bank, Sam shared what he'd witnessed with the Bradfords' rebuilt and refurnished homestead. When Emily would've excused herself to return to the mercantile, he murmured a request for her to stay.

And then he made his stand, facing his father across the expanse of the desk in his office, the woman he loved at his side.

"If there's one thing I've learned since I've been here, it's that life is about more than just profits. This community, these people," he shared a smile with Emily, "have something special. They're committed to each other. And it's my belief that together, they'll do more than survive—they'll thrive. You'd do better to find a way to incorporate the bank more deeply into the community instead of trying to tear the community apart piece by piece."

Sam's father appraised him. "Am I to assume this view comes from your association with this young lady?"

Sam couldn't be ashamed of the woman at his side. "Emily helped me see it, but my opinions are my own."

"It seems we have more to talk about than I thought. Will you have time to eat supper with me before heading out to your sister's place tonight?"

Sam nodded, then excused himself to walk Emily back.

~ * ~

Over supper at the hotel dining room, Sam's father seemed

to genuinely listen to what his son had to say about having a bank representative become more involved with the townspeople. Not only would it help them as they worked through difficult times, but also encourage them to try to pay their loans in a more timely fashion.

He didn't agree to the plan, but it was the first time Sam had ever felt he had his father's true consideration.

"If I decide to follow this plan of yours—which I'm not saying I will—are you open to being this *representative* for the Bank, for the family?"

Sam's chest expanded with pride. He let loose a breath he hadn't even realized he'd been holding. His father must've seen some worth in the work Sam had done in Bear Creek if he was considering giving him a job.

But he wasn't sure it was what he wanted. Not anymore. "I'd like a chance to think about it. To be honest, I've got some things to settle with Emily before I make a decision like that."

"What things?"

"I'm going to marry her, if she'll have me."

His father considered him for a long time, but in the end didn't respond to Sam's declaration.

As they parted after a final cup of coffee, his father gave Sam a rather awkward embrace, rather than the handshake he'd been expecting. It wasn't the full reconciliation Sam had hoped for when he'd started this job, but it was a start, something to build off of.

Now he needed to resolve things with Emily.

~ * ~

Sam's supper plans had changed for the meeting with his father, but he'd come for Emily soon after. The moon was bright above them as they walked slowly through the now-quiet town.

"Do you think your father will call in our loan?" she asked.

"I don't know." He looked over at her. "He was so quiet, I couldn't tell if he really heard what I had to say." He shifted, loosening her hold on his arm in order to twine their hands together. "But if he does, you won't be alone. Emily... I love you."

Her breath caught in her chest. They reached her porch, and he turned to face her, interlacing her other hand in his.

"I want to take care of you—and that includes your family, too. If we have to, we'll find a way to make it work. I've got some savings, and I thought we might invest in a homestead of our own—one close enough for you to walk to town so you could help your father in the store when he needs you."

"You mean—you're not going to keep working for your father?" Her mouth had gone so dry, she was surprised she could get the words out.

He chuckled. "I can't stand being in that office one more day. It's too confining. We'll get established, maybe even partner with my brother-in-law, if things work out." He ducked his head, the brim of his hat covering his eyes. "That is, if you feel the same."

"Oh, Sam." She took the initiative and reached up to touch his jaw. "I do love you."

He pressed his cheek to hers, and she heard the rattle in his breath as emotion overwhelmed him. "I started falling in love with you three years ago, when I was first working with Jonas."

She pushed back so she could see his face. "Really?"

He gave her a sheepish grin. "I thought it was a lost cause—because of Maxwell. That's why I left in such a hurry. I couldn't bear to be in love with my best friend's girl."

She shook her head. "And by then, Maxwell and I were just friends. What changed your mind now?"

Either she was imagining things, or his cheeks were coloring beneath his tan. "Oscar's been working on me for weeks to court you properly. But I was still afraid Maxwell might have feelings for you. So Oscar finally took it out of my hands—he sent a wire to his brother and got one back, telling me I was being a fool."

Now it was her turn to giggle. "I can only imagine"

"I tried—really tried—to stay away from you, to keep my

feelings in check, but... Emily, you're like the horseman on the other end of the lasso, for me. Everything about you drew me in—I couldn't help falling in love with you all over again, and I was a few hours away from making my declaration, whether or not I had Maxwell's blessing. My feelings for you are just too strong to hide anymore."

Emily's eyes filled with tears. He really did love her. She sniffled, giving a valiant attempt to hold back her emotions. "Then I suppose I just have one question left. How soon can you get a homestead set up?"

"I've got all the White boys on my side. How soon can you have a dress made?" he countered, eyes dancing.

"Soon," she promised. "Now I suppose you'd better get back to your father and conclude your business."

"Not yet," he murmured, and leaned down to kiss her—a seal for the promises they'd spoken and the ones to come.

EPILOGUE

"Isn't it time yet?" Sam asked from where he stood at the front of the small Bear Creek church. His tie threatened to choke off his air, and his palms were sweaty. He was as nervous as a green-broke horse with its first rider.

"Patience," murmured Oscar, who stood at his side. Maxwell hadn't been able to get away from school but had sent his best wishes in a long letter addressed to both Sam and Emily.

The church was filled with their family and friends. Even Sam's father looked relatively proud of his son. They'd made a somewhat tentative peace after the Bear Creek job had ended. Sam had managed to convince his father that working with the residents on their loans would be more successful than calling the loans, and so far his predictions had been right. With summer crops looking promising and the town banding together, the bank's profits were slowly improving. As was the status of Emily's family's store. When the townspeople had found out the mercantile was in trouble, they'd come through in a big way, many people making extra efforts to pay off the credit Mr. Sands had extended to them.

Sam's father had been grudgingly understanding when Sam had explained his need to work outdoors instead of taking the bank job his father had offered. Maybe Penny had helped pave the way for Sam—their parents had never expected her to marry or be happy with a simple homesteader, but after five years, her happiness hadn't dimmed.

"I still think it'll be your turn to get hitched soon," Sam

murmured to his friend.

"Not likely," Oscar laughed. "What woman is going to put up with an ornery cowhand like me?"

"When the right one comes along..." Sam forgot what he was saying the moment the outer door opened and Emily entered on her father's arm. Then he could barely remember his own name.

She was resplendent in a soft green dress that set off her golden hair and hazel eyes. Clutching a wildflower bouquet tightly to her stomach, she raised her eyes to meet his across the sanctuary.

Sam's own nervousness fled. He'd spent the last several years of his life wandering, missing the woman now walking toward him, until God had brought him back to Bear Creek and showed Sam the true dream of his heart.

He'd never take Emily for granted. Her love had changed him, changed his outlook and given direction to his life where he'd had none before.

This cowboy would be counting his blessings for decades to come.

ABOUT THE AUTHOR

USA Today bestselling author Lacy Williams works in a hostile environment (read: three-point-five kids age 6 and under). In spite of this, she has somehow managed to be a hybrid author since 2011, publishing 22 books & novellas. Lacy's books have finaled in the *RT Book Reviews* Reviewers' Choice Awards (2012, 2013, & 2014), the Golden Quill and the Booksellers Best Award. She is a member of American Christian Fiction Writers, Romance Writers of America and Novelists Inc.

Made in the USA
Las Vegas, NV
11 February 2021